James J Panerazio

The Man and
His Line

The Man and

His Line

Yoram

Ever-Hadani

Translated by Bertha Urdang

Fawcett Columbine   New York

Dedicated to everybody who has,
had, or will have a line, and
to the children of the Segev
district and its environs.
With Love.

A Fawcett Columbine Book
Published by Ballantine Books

Translation copyright © 1991 by Random House, Inc.

Library of Congress Catalog Card Number: 91-70733
ISBN: 0-449-90627-2

Design by Holly Johnson

Manufactured in the United States of America

First American Edition: November 1991
10 9 8 7 6 5 4 3 2 1

There once was a man who had a line.

The man and his line loved each other very much.

And so they went everywhere together.

Every morning the line would tickle

the man until he woke up . . .

And the man always woke up smiling.

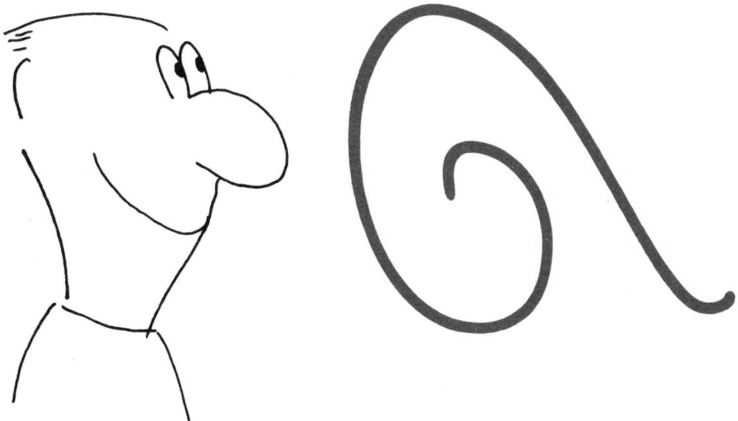

When a strong wind blew,
the man would tie the line to his
wrist.

After it rained

the man would hang up the line to dry.

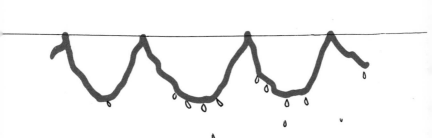

Sometimes they did not understand

one another.

And now and then

they even quarreled.

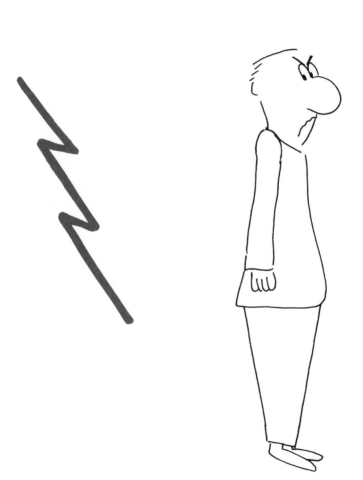

But in the end they always made up.

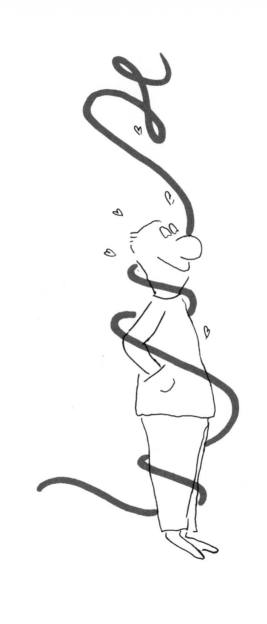

One day the man did not feel well,

so he went to bed.

But the line did not understand

what was happening.

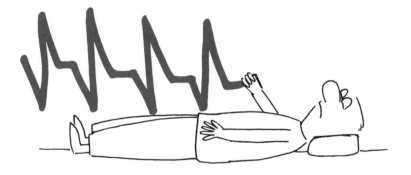

The line tried to tickle the man . . .

But he could not get him to laugh.

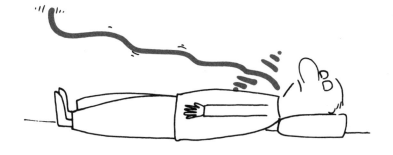

He tried to lift him . . .

But the man was too heavy.

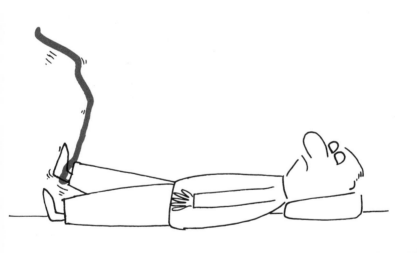

The line felt helpless,

so small and so sad.

The next day

the man opened his eyes a little

and the line was very, very happy.

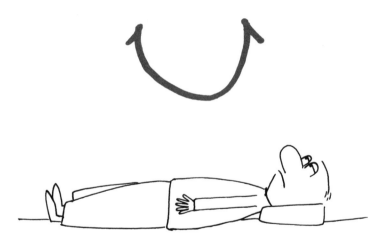

"I'm sick," said the man to the line,

but the line did not understand.

He tried to make the man laugh.

The man did smile, just a little.

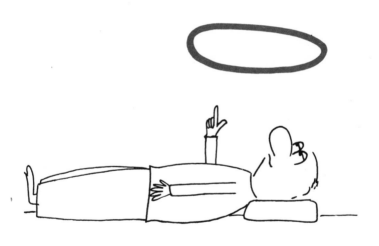

The following day

the man felt a little better

and was able to sit up in bed.

The line was even happier.

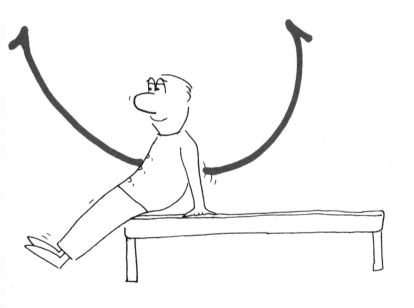

They went for a walk together.
The line was so happy that
he jumped for joy.

When they returned home

the man drank a big cup of tea.

The line wandered all over his nose.

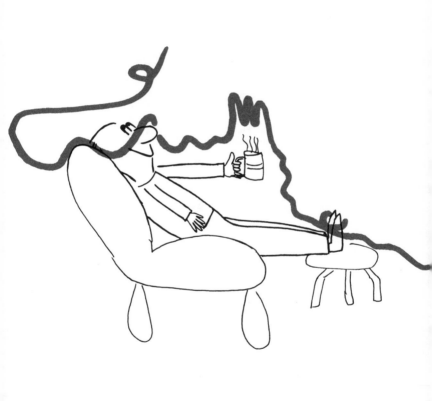

Later that day the line decided

to watch over the man

so that he would not fall ill again.

The man was happy that the line

was watching over him.

But he felt that it was harder

to move about easily.

At times the line got in his way.

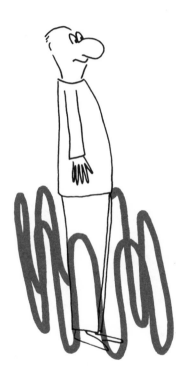

. . . After a few days

the man got fed up with

the line's constant watchfulness.

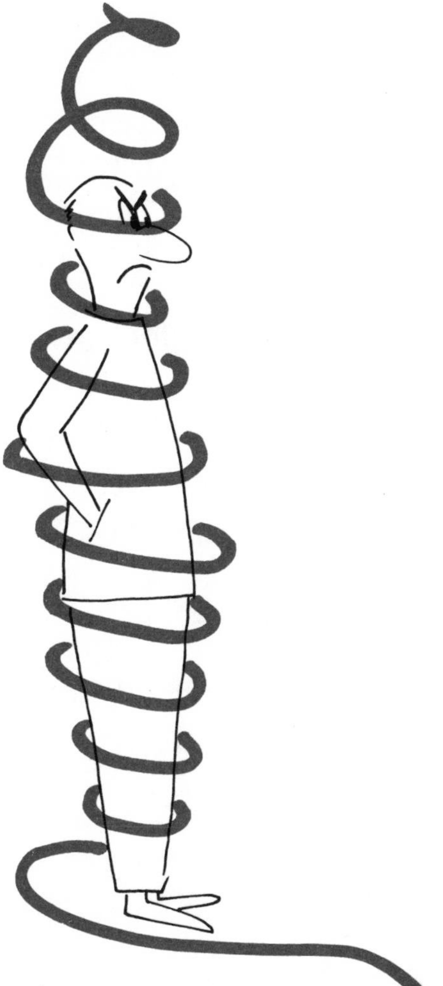

And the line also got a little tired

of looking after the man

who no longer laughed with him.

The line worried that maybe

the man did not love him

as much as before.

One day the man got so angry that he snapped the line in two and walked away.

. . . leaving the line on the floor.

And they did not meet again

for a long time.

One day while the man was strolling

down the street, he met another man

who was out with another line.

He began to long for his own line.

He felt very lonely.

"My line was much nicer," he thought.

He went on walking.

Suddenly he noticed something

dangling from a distant tree . . .

As he came nearer he recognized

his own line.

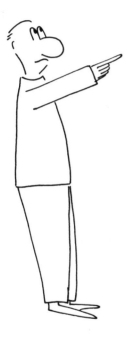

It was caught between the branches
of the tree and could not get free.

"Hello," said the man.

But the line was too weak to answer.

The man went up to the tree

and carefully untangled his line.

He wound it gently

and took it home with him.

The man

covered the line with a blanket,

and they both went to sleep.

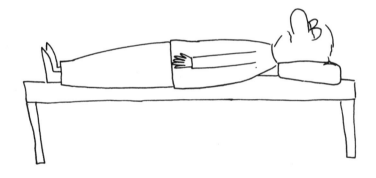

In the morning

the man felt a familiar tickle.

He thought he must be dreaming.

He turned over once,

then a second time,

and then he understood . . .

The line was feeling better.

He was waking the man up

just as he used to.

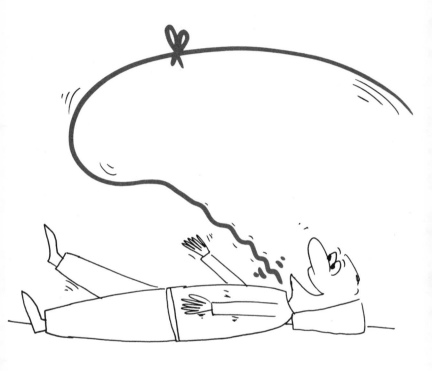

The man laughed

and laughed

and laughed

and laughed . . .

From then on, they were friends again.
But every time they noticed the knot
in the line, they remembered
what had happened to them.
And they were careful that it
should never happen again.

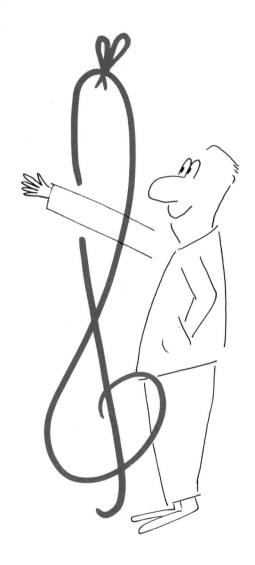

The end.